AUSTRALIAN LEGEND SERIES

THE TALE OF THE PLATYPUS

By L. & G. Adams
Illustrated by Murray McKenzie
Literature Consultant: Maurice Saxby

SRA

SCIENCE RESEARCH ASSOCIATES PTY. LTD.
Sydney, Chicago, Palo Alto, Toronto
Henley-on-Thames, Paris

A subsidiary of Science Research Associates, Inc.

Far beyond the great mountains which divide the seas from the plains, there flows a beautiful river.

Down in the plains it runs slow and wide. Up in the foothills, near the start of the river, it runs cool and clear and swift.

It was here in the hills, where the river banks were lined with lush ferns and rich green grass, that a tribe of platypus lived.

All day long the young ones splashed and played happily in the river. But whenever they swam too far from the safety of their home—the hole in the river bank—their mothers would warn them: "Don't swim too far down the river, or Mooroo will get you!"

The young ones were not exactly sure who Mooroo was, but the very mention of his name was enough to make them shiver with fright.

Now it happened that one day the skies grew black, and a big storm struck the hills. Very soon the river was turned into a raging torrent—racing along so fast that it swept away everything in its path.

Little Mokka, the young platypus, had been playing in the river when the storm struck. And now its bubbling, swirling waters caught him by surprise and quickly carried him down the river—far away from his warm and safe hole-in-the-bank.

On and on the racing river carried poor little Mokka, throwing him against passing logs and ducking him under as he tried to breathe. Then, as the raging waters swirled him around a big bend in the river, he was suddenly caught by the tangled branches of a large, overhanging tree. And there he stayed until the storm blew away and the river grew calm.

"I must swim back to my tribe," he told himself. "Or Mooroo will catch me."

Mokka was untangling himself from the branches when he saw someone swimming towards him.

"It's Mooroo," thought Mokka, "Mooroo!"

The stranger swam closer.

"Keep away from me, Mooroo" said Mokka rather nervously.

"Mooroo?" said the stranger. "I'm not Mooroo. I'm one of the duck tribe. But I know who you are. You're one of the platypus tribe."

"You're not Mooroo?" said little Mokka with relief. "Does Mooroo live near here?"

"Mooroo lives a little further down the river," said the old duck. "And you should not be here for fear he kills you!"

"Why would he want to kill me?" asked Mokka.

"Because he hasn't forgiven your ancestor for tricking him," said the wise old duck. "Come closer, and I will tell you how it happened."

Mokka swam over to the duck, who looked very old and very wise.

"For many years now," began the wise old duck. "For far more years than I can remember, our tribe has lived here at the bend in the river. Our days were always peaceful—as long as we never ventured down the river where a water devil might catch us.

"And we never ventured up the river, for there the water runs too fast. Even a duck may easily tire from swimming against the current and drown.

"We were happy enough living at bend-in-the-river. But one day a duck called Dana foolishly swam down the river in search of food. Soon she found a green, grassy bank.

"'Oh!' she thought. 'There must be some wonderful, big, juicy grubs to eat here.'

"So she forgot all the warnings about straying too far from bend-in-the-river. And she waddled off along the edge of the bank—happily eating the biggest and juiciest grubs she had ever seen.

"Dana was so busy finding grubs, that she almost fell into a big black hole. She was about to move on when she saw two tiny, orange lights shining deep down in the darkness.

"'What can those lights be?' she thought.

"As she watched, the lights began to grow larger and wider apart. She peered deeper into the hole. Suddenly she found herself staring right into the face of a big, ugly water-rat.

"The water-rat quickly sprang from the hole and grabbed Dana. Before she could even call out, he had tied her feet together.

"Dana screamed and yelled. But it was no use, for she was too far away from bend-in-the-river to be heard.

"Down, down, down into his hole he dragged her until at last they came to a great big room. This was the water-rat's home. It was dark and damp. The only furniture was a straw bed in one corner.

"'Now my beautiful little duck, I have you!' said the water-rat.

"'Oh, please let me go,' Dana cried. 'Please let me go back to my tribe.'

"'Never!' said the water-rat. 'Now that I have you, I am going to make you my wife.'

"On hearing this, Dana began to cry. So time went by, and day after day Dana was kept a prisoner of the water-rat, whose name was Mooroo.

"At first Dana did nothing but cry. But as time passed, she realized that crying would never help her escape. 'I must work out a plan if I am to escape,' she told herself.

"So Dana sat down in the corner and began to think hard.

"When Mooroo woke up the next morning, he was very surprised to find Dana happily preparing his breakfast. He was even more surprised when she said: 'Good morning, husband, I hope you slept well.'

"'Slept well?' said Mooroo with surprise. 'Wife, until today you have done nothing but cry. But this morning you seem happy. Why is this?'

"Dana answered: 'Mooroo, you have taken me from my tribe. At first that made me very sad. But now that I know you are a great hunter and a kind husband, I am happy to stay with you.'

"Mooroo, of course, was pleased to hear this.

"At first Mooroo was a little suspicious. But as time went on, he began to allow Dana more and more freedom. However, she was still not allowed to leave the hole. For whenever Mooroo went off to hunt, he always blocked the entrance with a huge stone—far too heavy for Dana to move.

"'I will lull Mooroo to sleep,' Dana thought, 'then he will forget to place the stone against the entrance.'

"So when Mooroo returned tired and hungry from his next hunting trip, Dana placed before him a big plate piled high with juicy grubs and yams and sweet berries.

"It was all Mooroo could do to force them down. Soon he had eaten so much that his stomach bulged.

"The heavy meal made Mooroo very tired. Within minutes his head was nodding. He fell asleep so quickly, he forgot to place the stone over the entrance.

"This was just what Dana had hoped would happen. Very quietly she tip-toed past the sleeping Mooroo.

"When she reached the entrance, she began to run as fast as her little legs could carry her—not even daring to look back in case she saw Mooroo close behind her.

"But the greedy Mooroo had eaten far too much to be
able to catch her.

"You can imagine how happy the duck tribe was to see Dana back at bend-in-the-river. "We thought you must have been killed!" they cried out.

"All the ducks gathered around Dana as she told them of her adventures and how she had escaped from Mooroo. That night there was a special party held in Dana's honour—a corroboree.

"Dana had been away for a whole year. It was spring again. And all the mother ducks were preparing nests to lay their eggs.

"Dana also built herself a comfortable nest and proudly laid two beautiful big eggs.

"How excited everyone was as all the eggs began to hatch. All, that is, except Dana's.

"'Hurry up and hatch your eggs, Dana,' the other ducks cried. 'We want to see your ducklings.'

"Then it happened. Dana jumped off the eggs, expecting to see two fluffy yellow ducklings.

"Instead, she saw two of the funniest looking animals
you could ever imagine. Instead of fluffy, yellow feathers,
they had a light sprinkling of fur covering their pink little
bodies. Instead of two legs, they had four.

"They had Dana's bill, and their feet were webbed just like hers. But their fur and four legs were just like those of their father—Mooroo.

"Now when the other ducks saw these strange looking creatures, they were horrified.

"'Take them away!' they screamed. 'They will frighten our babies!'

"Then a wise old drake came up to Dana and said: 'You must take your children away from bend-in-the-river, for they are not of the duck tribe.'

"'But where will I go?' cried Dana.

"'You must go up the river,' said the drake. 'If you go down the river, Mooroo will kill your children, for they are not of the water-rat tribe either.'

"So Dana called her children and took them far up the river. She was sad. But her children followed her happily.

"Finally they reached the foothills where the river ran cool and clear and swift. And here they made their new home. They called themselves the platypus tribe.

"Soon they were happy once again. And the beautiful river in the hills became their tribal ground.

"You must be of that tribe," said the wise old duck to Mokka. "Look at you. Although you have a duck's bill and webbed feet, you have four legs and fur—just like the water-rat. That is why you must not go further down the river, or Mooroo will catch you."

The mention of Mooroo's name made Mokka shiver. Suddenly he remembered his mother and his own tribe back at hole-in-the-bank.

Quickly saying goodbye to the wise old duck, Mokka swam off towards his home as fast as he could.

He swam for hours and hours until he thought he could go no further. But none of the river banks looked familiar.

"Maybe I'm lost," he thought. Then, as he rounded a bend, he suddenly saw a big old log.

"I've seen that log before," he thought. And there, just beyond it, was his very own hole-in-the-bank.

How excited all the platypus tribe were to see him.

"We thought Mooroo had caught you," said his tearful mother as she kissed him and stroked his fur.

"I did not see Mooroo," said Mokka, who was overjoyed to be back home. "But I did see the wise old duck who lives at bend-in-the-river."

Then all the happy platypus tribe gathered around Mokka to hear about his great adventure.